Waves in the Bathtub

Eugenie Fernandes

Scholastic Canada Ltd.

2

Last night,
when Mother put Kady into the bathtub,
waves began to appear.
Just little waves at first.
But then the waves got bigger,
and BIGGER,
and BIGGER!
And Kady sang the bathtub song.

Imagining the ocean,
I can see
waves in the bathtub
here with me.

4

I see creatures big and small.

Lots of fish! I like them all.

I like polar bears

in my tub,

dolphins and pelicans,

scrub-a-dub-a-dub.

"I like the ocean," said Kady.
"So do I," said Mother,
"but please keep it in the tub,
and don't forget to scrub your toes."

Kady did not want to scrub her toes.
She wanted to play.
So the waves in the tub got bigger,
and BIGGER,
and BIGGER,
and then Kady sang the bathtub song again.

Imagining the ocean, I can see
waves in the bathtub here with me.
I see creatures big and small.
Lots of fish! I like them all.
I like penguins in my tub,

walrus and octopus,

scrub-a-dub-a-dub.

Mother said, "It's getting late.
Time to go to bed."

But Kady did not want to go to bed.
She wanted to splash,
so the waves in the tub got bigger,
and BIGGER,
and BIGGER,
and then Kady sang the bathtub song again.

Imagining the ocean, I can see
waves in the bathtub here with me.

I see creatures big and small.
Lots of fish! I like them all.

I like sea otters

in my tub,

big whales and little snails,

scrub-a-dub-a-dub.

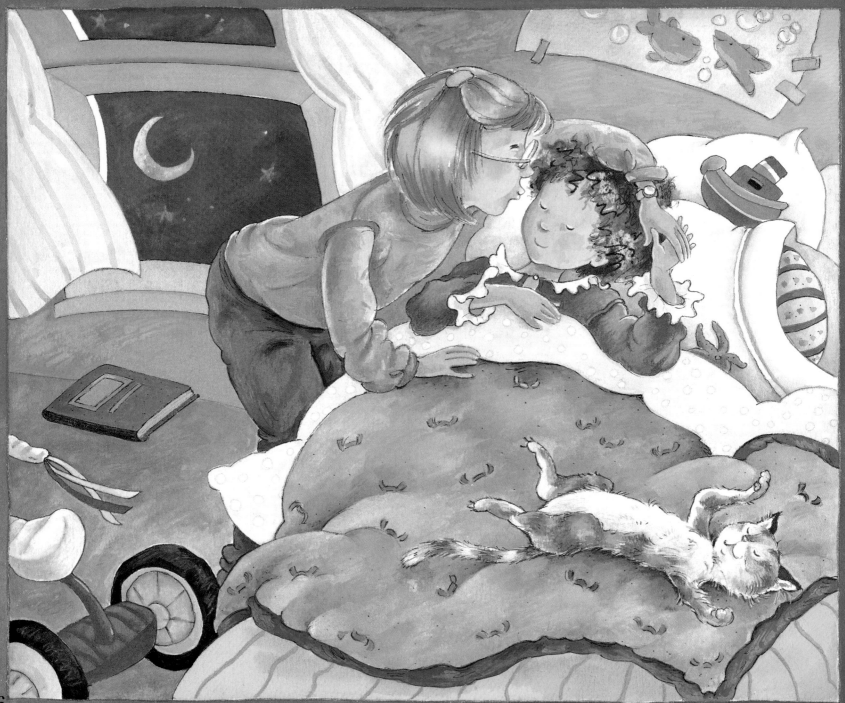

Mother took Kady out of the tub
and dried her off
and put her to bed
and read her a story
and kissed her goodnight
and turned out the light
and kissed her again
and guess what Mother did then?

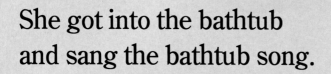

She got into the bathtub
and sang the bathtub song.

Imagining the ocean, I can see
waves in the bathtub here with me.
I see creatures big and small.
Lots of fish! I like them all.
I like the ocean in my tub,
splashing and bubbling,
scrub-a-dub-a-dub!

29

The Bathtub Song

Im - ag - in - ing the o - cean I can see   waves in the bath tub here with me.

I   see creat - ures big and small   Lots of fish! I   like them all.

I like pol - ar bears in my tub   dol - phins and pel - i - cans scrub - a - dub - a - dub!

These are some of the verses of the bathtub song. You can make up your own, too!

1. polar bears . . . dolphins and pelicans
2. penguins . . . walrus and octopus

3. sea otters . . . big whales and little snails
4. the ocean . . . splashing and bubbling

For Peter

*The illustrations for this book were done in watercolour
and gouache, with pen and watercolour pencils.*

Canadian Cataloguing in Publication Data

Fernandes, Eugenie, 1943-
   Waves in the bathtub

ISBN 0-590-24343-8

I.Title.

PS8561.E75W38 1994   jc813'.54   C94-930897-8
PZ7.F47Wa 1994

6 5 4 3 2   Printed in Hong Kong   5 6 7 8/9